Elliot's Park

The Walnut Cup

BY PATRICK CARMAN
ILLUSTRATED BY STEVE JAMES

Orchard Books
An Imprint of Scholastic Inc. ✦ New York

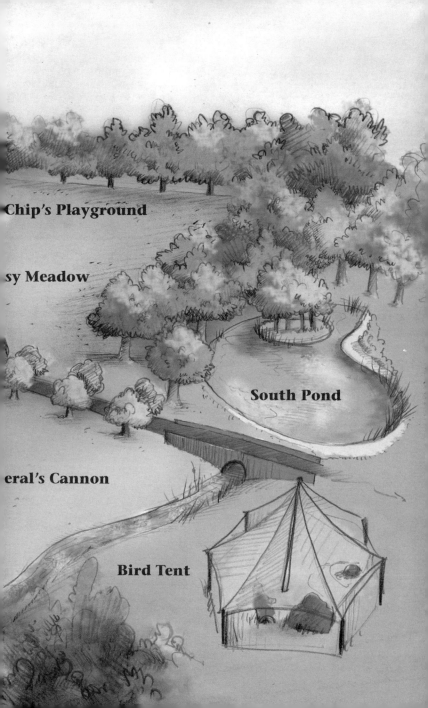

Chip's Playground

sy Meadow

South Pond

eral's Cannon

Bird Tent

For Reece Carman and Ken Geist,
two people who love Elliot's Park
as much as I do!

Text copyright © 2009 by Patrick Carman. • Interior illustrations copyright © 2009 by Steve James. • Map illustration copyright © 2009 by Squire Broel. All rights reserved. Published by Orchard Books, an imprint of Scholastic Inc., *Publishers since 1920*. ORCHARD BOOKS and design are registered trademarks of Watts Publishing Group, Ltd., used under license. SCHOLASTIC and associated logos are trademarks and/or registered trademarks of Scholastic Inc. No part of this publication may be reproduced, stored in a retrieval system, or transmitted in any form or by any means, electronic, mechanical, photocopying, recording, or otherwise, without written permission of the publisher. For information regarding permission, write to Orchard Books, Scholastic Inc., Permissions Department, 557 Broadway, New York, NY 10012.

ISBN-13: 978-0-545-01939-2 • ISBN-10: 0-545-01939-7

10 9 8 7 6 5 4 3 2 1   09 10 11 12 13

Printed in the U. S. A.   40 • First edition, April 2009

Art type digital • Cover illustration copyright © 2009 by Jim Madsen.

Book design by Lillie Mear

CHAPTERS

CHAPTER 1

The Teams Arrive!

Flowers were beginning to bloom. Birds were singing. The grass had turned bright green. It was spring in Elliot's Park! And that meant something BIG was about to happen.

"Bravo! Here comes the team from Brazil!" shouted Crash in her British accent.

Elliot looked up in the air and saw Crash flying overhead. Crash was the only flying squirrel in the park.

"Where?" cried Elliot. "I don't see them."

"And the German team! And the Italian team! And the Swedish team! And the —" she continued.

But Crash wasn't watching where she was going. She flew right into the branches of a big tree. It made a lot of noise.

"Are you all right?" cried Elliot from below. The branches moved back and forth above him. They were filled with tiny new leaves. Crash's head poked out into the open.

"Jolly good!"

Elliot's best friend, Chip, was coming toward them. He was dribbling a walnut between his feet. Chip kicked it *really* hard and *really* high and it went sailing into the tree. Crash dodged the walnut but lost her balance and fell backward. When Elliot looked up, Crash was hanging by one paw.

"I see our captain has arrived," Crash said. Her flying goggles were crooked on her nose.

Chip smiled and retrieved the walnut.

They were all dressed in bright red, white, and blue Elliot's Park soccer jerseys.

"Let's go welcome the teams to the park," said Elliot.

"This year we're going to win it all!" said Chip. Chip liked to win things. He was the captain of the team. But Elliot wasn't so sure. A lot of great teams came to the Walnut Cup.

"Do you really think we can win?" asked Elliot. Chip bounced the walnut between his little knees as they walked.

"Are you kidding? We're the best team ever!"

Chip let the walnut hit the ground. He kicked it *really* hard and *really* high again. It sailed out into the open and landed on the far end of the soccer field. One of the Brazilians flicked it into the air. It bounced off his head, his heel, his knee, and then to one of his teammates. The walnut went back and forth between them. All the Brazilians laughed.

"Tricky footwork," said Elliot.

"Nothing we can't handle," said Chip.

Crash flew low and tumbled over and over again across the field. She did about ten flips and came to a stop. The rest of the Elliot's Park team was already on the field practicing: Sparkle, Pistachio, Stitches, and Elliot's sister, Twitch.

Twitch was bouncing up and down. Her lips were orange.

"You've been drinking soda pop, haven't you?" asked Elliot.

Twitch nodded. Then she burped. It was an orange-flavored burp. She was very happy.

Elliot turned his attention to the visiting teams. Brazil, Germany, Sweden, and Italy were already kicking walnuts all over the field. France, Japan, and Spain were just arriving. Including Elliot's team, that made eight teams. And there were six squirrels on every team. It was a lot of squirrels!

"Welcome to the Walnut Cup!" said Elliot. "The tournament begins in one hour!"

Everyone cheered. Squirrels love soccer.

"And de game ball? Where is de game ball?" asked one of the Brazilians. The home team had to provide a *perfectly* round walnut. It was a rule. If Elliot didn't have one, the

12

teams wouldn't be allowed to play. They'd all lose before they even started!

Chip still had the same walnut he'd been kicking all over the park. One of the German players stepped forward. He was looking at the walnut.

"Das is ze game ball?" he asked.

The two strikers for the Swedish team also inspected the walnut. Their names were Sven and Olga.

"Shape like egg," said Sven.

"Must be *round*."

The Italians also piped in.

"Where is round ball? And spaghetti.

Where
is the
spaghetti?"

The Italians
loved pasta.

"Not to worry!" said
Elliot. "I have a *very*
round walnut for the
tournament. I've been saving it all winter
just for today. It's *perfect*!"

Everyone began to practice while Elliot
ran home to get the *perfectly* round walnut.
It was hidden in his tree house. Little did
Elliot know that someone was secretly
following him. It was someone who LOVED
walnuts even more than soccer. Someone
who'd been listening and watching from
high up in a tree. It was a squirrel named
Pistachio!

CHAPTER 2

Stolen!

A perfectly round walnut was hard to find. All summer long Elliot had searched and searched until finally he'd found it. Actually, it had found him. The perfectly round walnut had fallen from a tree and bonked Elliot on the head.

When Elliot arrived at the door to his tree house he looked back at the field. Walnuts were flying everywhere! All the teams were warming up. Headers! Passes! Drop kicks! Almost fifty squirrels zipping and zooming in their brightly colored uniforms.

Elliot could hardly wait to get back and test out the perfectly round walnut. He went inside his tree house and moved his comfy chair. Behind the chair was a box. Inside the box was another box. And inside that box he found the hidden walnut.

"WOW. What a perfectly round walnut! It's the best I've ever seen!"

Elliot was very proud of his little treasure. He knew how important it was.

"Boy, am I thirsty," he said.

Elliot set the perfectly round walnut on his comfy chair. He filled his cup with lemonade (squirrels love lemonade). When he turned back to his chair, the perfectly round walnut was gone.

"Where's my walnut?"

Elliot thought maybe it had rolled off the chair. He looked under the bed, the sink, and the table. But there was no walnut. Then he stepped out onto the limb in front of his door.

"Hey!!" he cried. From there he could see where the perfectly round walnut had gone. "Pistachio! Come back with my walnut!"

Pistachio LOVED nuts more than almost anything.

The perfectly round walnut was tucked under Pistachio's paw. He was running through the park as fast as he could.

"Come back here!" yelled Elliot. "That's the game ball!"

But Pistachio just kept running. Elliot didn't know what to do. If he lost the game ball the teams wouldn't be allowed to play. They'd all be standing on sidelines!

Pistachio was getting farther away. He was heading toward the pond.

Crash and Chip were warming up on the soccer field. They heard all the yelling and wondered what was going on.

"You better go find Elliot," said Chip. "It sounds like he's in trouble."

Crash could race across the park faster than any other squirrel. She was *super* fast when she flew. It was the slowing down part that was hard for her.

Crash dashed up the side of a tree. She ran across a long limb. She jumped into the air. And, before you could say "spaghetti" three times fast, she was almost at Elliot's front door!

"You're going too fast!" said Elliot. He said this a lot when Crash was trying to land.

Crash sailed through with a *wooooosh*! There was a lot of noise inside. When Elliot looked into his tree house the table was turned over. His chair was on its side. The lemonade had spilled.

"Might I be of service?" said Crash. She stood and shook the lemonade out of her tail.

"Pistachio stole the game ball!" yelled Elliot. "You have to stop him before he breaks it open and eats it!"

"You don't say," said Crash. She was a calm sort of squirrel.

Crash went to the door. She looked out over the park and saw Pistachio running.

"He's a crafty one, but I think I can catch him."

Crash flapped her arms. She adjusted her goggles.

"Tallyhoooooooo!"

And with that, Crash jumped into the air and took chase. She sailed *super* fast over the park. All the teams on the field saw her. And they saw Pistachio run past with the game ball.

"You can catch him, Crash!" said Chip. He ran after Pistachio. All the teams ran after Pistachio. Every squirrel in the park was running after Pistachio! Everyone but Crash — she was flying right over his head. She had caught up.

Pistachio was almost at the pond. There was a nice big rock at the edge that was good for breaking open walnuts. Pistachio had used it many times. He could see the big rock! And right past that was the glassy water of the pond.

"Cheerio!" said Crash. She made her final dive. Pistachio looked back and saw everyone chasing him. Then he looked up

and . . . *CRASH*! The flying
squirrel landed on top of him. They
tumbled over and over and over again.
Pistachio couldn't hold on to the perfectly
round walnut.

Phwooooop!

The perfectly round walnut popped free
and into the air. It sailed over the big rock.

"NO!" cried Elliot. He was way behind
everyone else, but catching up fast. He could
see the walnut flying through the air.

Elliot's perfectly round walnut sailed all
the way over the pond and landed in the
water with a big *PLOP*!

When Pistachio and Crash stopped rolling,
they both looked up.

"Got him!" said Crash.

All the visiting teams started yelling. It was a disaster!

"Nice going, Pistachio!" said Chip.

"Where is spaghetti?" asked one of the Italian players. He was hungry.

"No ball, no game!" said one of the Germans.

All the teams had their own egg-shaped walnuts to practice with. But they couldn't use one of those for the biggest soccer tournament of the year. Egg-shaped walnuts were fine for practice, but not for big games. They wobbled! Unless Elliot could find a perfectly round walnut — and fast! — the Walnut Cup was sure to be canceled.

CHAPTER 3

Rules by
Referee Ranger Canyon

Ranger Canyon was standing on
a box in the middle of the field. He was the
referee, and he took his job seriously. All the
teams were crowded around.

"I have here an *almost* perfectly round walnut," said Referee Ranger Canyon. He was holding the best walnut Elliot could find on short notice. It was shaped like a party balloon.

"Which means . . ." said Referee Ranger Canyon.

Elliot tried to plug his ears. He closed his eyes very tightly. But it was no use. He could still hear Ranger Canyon.

"The Walnut Cup is canceled!"

"What! But that walnut *is* round!" said Chip. He had practiced all winter. There was no way Chip was going to miss the Walnut Cup.

"Just look at it! It's round," said Chip.

"Das valnut looks like an egg," said one of the German players. All the other teams nodded.

"The league rules are clear!" cried Referee Ranger Canyon. "The Walnut Cup can only be played with a perfectly *round* walnut."

Referee Ranger Canyon looked at his watch. "Forty-five minutes to the first whistle. Find that walnut!"

All of the Elliot's Park players walked off the field. They were heartbroken. If they couldn't find a new ball in forty-five minutes, the Walnut Cup was off!

Daisy, Autumn, and Lefty were the cheerleaders. They tried to cheer up Elliot and the rest of the team with a cheer. They

even pinched the mascot's ear so he would speak. The mascot was Mister Nibbles, a stuffed squirrel.

"Hello! My name is Mister Nibbles! What is your name?" said Mister Nibbles. The things he said didn't always make sense. But Mister Nibbles had a squeaky voice that usually made everyone laugh.

The team wasn't cheered up. They sat down and started complaining.

"All that practice for nothing!" yelled Chip.

"This is the pits!" said Sparkle.

"We really blew it this time!" Twitch hiccupped.

"What are we going to do?" asked Stitches. She was the park doctor.

And there was one little squirrel who watched everything. He was hiding up in

a tree, too afraid to come down. He felt
terrible.

It was Pistachio. He watched the Elliot's
Park team as they walked off the field. He
saw how disappointed they were. And it
wasn't just Elliot's team. All the teams were
disappointed. Pistachio had really let his love
of walnuts get him in trouble this time. In
fact, it had gotten everyone in trouble. He
had never expected that!

"I can't let this happen," said Pistachio. "I
have to get that walnut back."

And so Pistachio ran down the side of the tree. He ran right past the Elliot's Park team.

"Where's *he* going?" said Chip.

"I'm getting that nut back!" said Pistachio as he ran off.

"Wait up! We'll help," called Elliot.

All the teams raced after Pistachio.

Pistachio ran faster than he'd ever run before. And he didn't stop when he came to the edge of the pond. He jumped!

"Pistachio!" cried Elliot and his friends. They'd never seen anything like it. Squirrels don't jump in the water. They don't like wet fur. And besides, they can't swim very well.

"Pistachio! Come back!" cried Stitches. "Come back!"

Pistachio was dog-paddling as fast as he could, and all the teams ran for the pond. A dog-paddling squirrel is a very rare sight. So rare that it caught the attention of Wilma, the biggest — and the meanest — goose in the pond!

Honk! Honk! Honk!

Wilma could really honk.

"Watch out, Pistachio!" cried Twitch and Sparkle. Poor little Pistachio was all wet. He was paddling as hard as he could. And he was being chased by Wilma! All of the other teams looked on in wonder.

"That is very big goose," said one of the Japanese players.

"Forget the walnut!" cried Elliot. "Get back here!"

But Pistachio had the nut and held on tightly.

"He really wants that walnut," said Chip.

All the teams yelled and cheered from the edge of the pond.

"Bring that nut back!"

Chip thought better of Pistachio then. "You can do it, Pistachio! Don't give up!"

What a scene on the pond! Wilma was close behind. Pistachio was getting farther and farther from shore.

"You're going the wrong way!" yelled Elliot.

All the other teams watched the excitement. They'd never seen anything like it.

"Is very entertaining," said one of the French players. Everyone agreed.

Wilma had caught up!

Honk! Honk! Honk!

She was snapping her big beak right behind Pistachio's tail. It was awful!

"He's headed for the island," said Crash. "I think he's going to make it!"

There was a small island in the middle of the pond. And sure enough, Pistachio did make it. Wilma followed him ashore and took chase. She could waddle really fast. But Pistachio was even faster. Pistachio was zooming up the side of one of the island's trees.

"He made it!" said Chip. "Wow! What a chase!"

Honk! Honk! Honk!

Wilma was not happy. This was her island and squirrels were not allowed.

Pistachio stood on a limb, dripping wet and shaking. He was breathing really hard, trying to catch his breath. Then he smiled a big smile and held the perfectly round walnut over his head. He wobbled and almost fell over.

"Stay where you are!" cried Elliot. "We'll save you!"

But no one had ever been stranded on the island before. Everyone looked at Elliot, even the players from the other teams.

Elliot was the smartest squirrel in the park. They all expected him to have a plan. But he didn't have a plan! The Walnut Cup was going to start in only thirty minutes. He had to save Pistachio *and* the game ball. And fast!

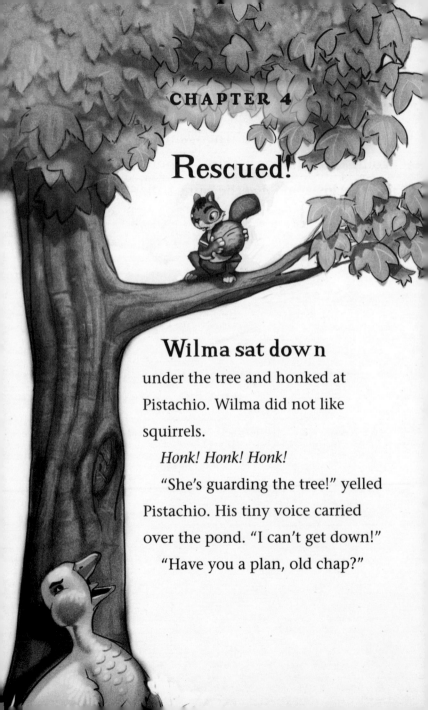

CHAPTER 4

Rescued!

Wilma sat down
under the tree and honked at
Pistachio. Wilma did not like
squirrels.

Honk! Honk! Honk!

"She's guarding the tree!" yelled
Pistachio. His tiny voice carried
over the pond. "I can't get down!"

"Have you a plan, old chap?"

asked Crash. She was staring at Elliot. Everyone was staring at Elliot.

"Ummmm. Yes! I have a plan. I'll be right back!"

Elliot ran away. He ran past the Italians, the Brazilians, the French, the Swedish, the Japanese, the Spanish, and the Germans.

"Ver dos he go to?" asked one of the German players.

"Don't worry," said Chip. "Elliot is very smart. He has a plan. He always does."

Except Elliot didn't have a plan. He rarely did. So instead, he ran between two big bushes to a little tree. It was the tree where Scratchy Spurs lived. Scratchy Spurs was the oldest, wisest squirrel in the park. He scratched a lot.

"Scratchy Spurs! I'm in trouble!"

But Scratchy Spurs didn't hear anything. If he wasn't scratching, he was sleeping. When Elliot found him, he was sleeping.

"How can you sleep at a time like this!" cried Elliot. "Pistachio is stranded on the island! We've no game ball! It's a disaster!"

Elliot picked up the twig lying across Scratchy's lap — his cane — and tickled the bottom of the old squirrel's foot. Scratchy

Spurs didn't wake up, so Elliot picked up a really BIG round stick and held it over his head. He was just about to bonk Scratchy Spurs on the noggin with it. But then he stopped.

He looked at the big round stick. He looked at the cane.

"I think I have a plan!"

Elliot smiled from ear to ear.

"Wow! Thanks, Scratchy Spurs!"

But Elliot's old friend didn't hear him. He was still sleeping.

Elliot looked around on the ground until he found a small stick like Scratchy's cane. Then he carried the big round stick and the small, flat stick back to the pond. He gathered all the players from all the teams.

"I'm going to need everyone to help me. Can we work together?"

A chorus of yes! yes! yes! in every language filled the air.

"Sí! Ja! Oui! Jo! Sim! Hai! Sì!"

"I can't understand a word they're saying," said Chip. "I think they want something to eat."

"You show them what to do, Chip," said Elliot. "I need a *di-ver-sion*. A big one!

"I'm going over there," said Elliot. He was pointing to the island. "And I need Wilma to go over there." He pointed to the other end of the pond.

Chip rubbed his head and thought really hard. After about three minutes he yelled. "I've got it!" Chip called all his teammates close. "Come on! Follow me."

Then Chip ran away. He ran all the way to the other side of the pond. He took the balloon-shaped walnut with him.

"Catch!" he cried. Then he kicked the walnut *really* hard and *really* high. It sailed over the water. Higher and farther it went! Until it landed in the open arms of Sven. He passed the ball to his teammate Olga. Then Olga kicked the walnut back over the pond. And the ball landed right near Wilma's house! Chip raced to the goose's house to get the ball back.

And then Elliot heard a wonderful sound.

Honk! Honk! Honk!

Wilma was swimming toward Chip and away from the island! Before long she was in the middle of a game of keep-away with the squirrels. Back and forth went the ball, everyone taking a turn. And back and forth went Wilma, honking and swimming.

"Now, Elliot! This is your chance!" yelled Chip.

"Have a go at it!" Crash piped in.

Elliot threw the big round stick in the water. Then he jumped in after it. He sat right on top of the big round stick. It was wobbly and his paws were in the water, but it worked! He had the small, flat stick in his front paws. It was his oar.

"Row, row, row," said Elliot.

Honk! Honk! Honk!

"Paddle faster! I think I hear Wilma coming!" said Pistachio. He was climbing down out of the tree while carefully holding on to the perfectly round walnut.

"Row, row, row," said Elliot. He arrived at the island, and Pistachio jumped on board with the perfectly round walnut.

"Don't drop the walnut!" said Elliot.

But Pistachio had something else on his mind.

"Paddle faster! She's coming back!"

Elliot didn't look back. He didn't have to. He could hear Wilma's honks getting closer.

Honk! Honk! Honk!

"She's right behind us!" said Pistachio.

Elliot kept paddling and paddling. They were almost to the shore. The game of keep-away had ended and everyone was cheering them on.

"Go, Elliot! Go!"

They were almost there. Only a few feet to go!

Elliot heard a *snap*! When he looked in his paws, the paddle was gone. Wilma had chomped down on the small flat stick and pulled it out of his hands.

"Oh, no!" he cried.

Elliot and Pistachio were so scared they jumped to their feet. They ran and ran and

ran. But they didn't go anywhere. The log spun and spun and spun on the water. They were running in place.

HONK!

Wilma let out the biggest honk yet.

"Woooohooooo!" yelled Elliot and Pistachio. They jumped off the big round stick and zoomed across the last little bit of water.

All the teams cheered and cheered. It was a worldwide celebration!

"Where's the perfectly round walnut?" said Chip.

"Right here!" said Pistachio. He held it out to Ranger Canyon.

"It's a little bit wet," said Referee Ranger Canyon. "But it's perfectly round. The tournament is on!"

"And just in time," said Chip. He was excited to take the field.

"Let the Walnut Cup begin!"

CHAPTER 5

Play Ball!

"Pass it! Pass it!" yelled Sparkle.
She was right in front of the goal. Elliot
kicked the ball as hard as he could. It sailed
into the air. Chip bonked it with his head
and it sailed even higher.

"Here it comes!" said Elliot.

"I've got it!" said Stitches. And she did get it! She dribbled past Sven. She passed to Sparkle. Sparkle dribbled past Olga. She passed back to Stitches.

And then BOOM! Stitches shot the perfectly round walnut right past the Swedish goalie!

"SCOOOOOORE!" yelled Referee Ranger Canyon.

Twitch was the Elliot's Park goalie. She bounced up and down at the other end of the field. Stitches and Sparkle were her best friends, so she was very excited. Plus, she'd had a raspberry-flavored pop before the game.

"Way to — *hiccup* — go! Way to go!" she cried. *Hiccup*. Her pop-top necklace jingled loudly as she jumped.

The Walnut Cup went on all day long. All the teams played super hard. At the very end, Referee Ranger Canyon called everyone together in the middle of the field. It was time for the awards ceremony.

"To all our guests from far away, thank you for visiting Elliot's Park," said Referee Ranger Canyon. "You're all winners to us!"

Everyone cheered. Ranger Canyon put his paws up to quiet the crowd. Then he announced the results.

"In first place," said Ranger Canyon. "The Brazilians!"

The Brazilians were a crowd favorite. They smiled a lot and always had fun on the field. Scratchy Spurs stopped scratching long enough to let out a *woooohooooo*! Even old squirrels love to cheer the Brazilians.

"Way to go Brazil!" cheered Autumn, Lefty, and Daisy.

"You are my best friend!" said the mascot, Mister Nibbles.

Referee Ranger Canyon quieted the crowd again.

"In second place," he said, "the Germans!"

More cheering. Everyone liked the Germans. They played great defense.

"And in third," said Referee Ranger Canyon, "our own Elliot's Park team!"

All the teams and all the fans cheered super loud. The game ball had been perfect. The field had been perfect. All the teams had a lot of fun. The Walnut Cup was an international hit!

As soon as the cheering stopped, one of the Italians tapped Elliot on the shoulder.

"Where is spaghetti?"

Elliot finally had an answer the Italian liked.

"Right this way!"

It had been a long day of soccer. The time to eat had finally come.

When everyone was seated at the long table, Referee Ranger Canyon stood.

"Every year the game ball is awarded to the most valuable player," he said. "And this

year the most valuable player helped more than just his own team."

Everyone nodded. They all knew who Referee Ranger Canyon was talking about.

"For helping all the teams work together," he said. He held the perfectly round walnut over his head. "And for saving the game ball," he continued, "I am proud to award this walnut to . . .

"Elliot!"

Everyone clapped and chirped. Elliot bowed and took the perfectly round walnut. Then he looked at Pistachio. It had been a long day for his friend.

"You made a mistake, but then you tried to fix it," said Elliot. "And that's a hard thing to do."

He held out the walnut. Pistachio smiled a very big smile. He had only one thing on his mind. Pistachio took the walnut. He ran as fast as he could to the big rock. He broke the perfectly round walnut open. Then he raced back to the table.

Pistachio took a big bite of walnut and passed it on.

"Let's all share what's inside," he said.

And so they did.

Elliot looked out over the long table. He loved his park more than ever. He slurped a long piece of spaghetti, and the Italians laughed.

"Next year, you come to Italy. We have real spaghetti!"

Elliot thought that sounded fun. But for now, he was happy to stay right where he was. At the best park in the whole wide world!

CAST OF

Chip

Chip is a bit bigger than other squirrels and he loves

all kinds of sports. He has a history of major accidents, including the time he chipped one of his two large front teeth on the monkey bars. Chip is a daredevil and will try anything. *Distinguishing features: two large front teeth, one chipped; Elliot's best friend.*

Crash

Crash is the only flying squirrel in Elliot's Park. She has trouble with her landing skills. She says she is

only stopping by on a planned flight around the world. But she always has a good reason for staying. Crash loves to tell about all the places she's been.

Distinguishing features: the only flying squirrel of the

CHARACTERS

bunch; British accent, flying goggles, and often has trouble landing.

Daisy, Autumn, and Lefty

All three are young, resourceful, and highly

competitive scouts. They are always performing tasks to earn Canyon Squirrel Scout merit badges. *Distinguishing features: bright blue merit badge vests.*

Elliot

Elliot is a very smart squirrel who lives inside the largest tree in the park. Whenever a problem arises, Elliot solves it,

with the help of his friends. A lovable nerd. *Distinguishing features: big black glasses; he usually wears a collared shirt with a wide tie.*

Mister Nibbles

Mister Nibbles is not an ordinary squirrel; he's a stuffed animal squirrel. When you press his ear he says five different things. All the other squirrels in the park think Mister Nibbles is hilarious. *Distinguishing features: stuffed; he does not move and says only five things.*

Pistachio

Pistachio is a nut lover. He will forcibly take nuts from anyone who enters the park eating them. He is often seen being chased up a tree by parents and dogs. *Distinguishing features: always eating, hiding, or trying to open a nut of one kind or another.*

Ranger Canyon

Canyon is the Park Ranger squirrel, also a Squir-

rel Scout leader. He gives out merit badges to Squirrel Scouts for completing park assignments. *Distinguishing features: a Park Ranger tie and a handle-*

bar mustache.

Roscoe and Coconut

Roscoe and Coconut are two giant dogs that

live across the street from El-liot's Park in the yellow house. They love to escape from the yard and run into the park to chase the squirrels.

Roscoe and Coconut also love to bark. *Distinguish-ing features: Roscoe is jet-black, Coconut is all white; neither has had a bath in a very long time.*

Scratchy Spurs

Scratchy Spurs is a retired rodeo squirrel who dreams

 of riding one last time. He is the oldest and wisest squirrel in Elliot's Park. Scratchy Spurs and Elliot are buddies. Scratchy Spurs scratches himself a lot.

Distinguishing features: spurs, battered cowboy hat, grass in mouth, twig cane; he speaks with a southern accent.

Sparkle

Sparkle loves stars and stargazing. She likes to be out

 at night. Sparkle is always getting in trouble with the owls. She likes to sleep in late and sometimes misses breakfast and lunch. *Distinguishing feature: star-shaped earrings.*

Stitches

Stitches is the park doctor. She is especially well liked by everyone. *Distinguishing features: white coat and a stethoscope around her neck.*

Twitch

Twitch is Elliot's sister. She loves any type of sugar,

especially soda pop of any flavor. She is very good at finding soda pop. She is hyper almost all of the time. *Distinguishing features: jangling soda pop–top*

necklace; runs around a lot and is very good at burping.

Wilma

Wilma is the biggest goose in the pond in Elliot's

Park. She does not like anyone, especially squirrels. *Distinguishing features: big, white, and loves to honk.*

Elliot's High-Energy Apple Surprise

Playing soccer all day can really make a squirrel hungry! But Elliot has the perfect snack for after a game. And it's so easy, you can make your own!

What you'll need for this snack:

- An apple
- An apple corer
- A grown-up
- A spoon
- Peanut butter
- Raisins
- M&M'S (optional)

To make Elliot's delicious snack, follow the simple steps below.

1. Wash and dry your apple.

2. Using the apple corer, remove the core of your apple. *(Always have a grown-up help you with this step!)*

3. Make sure to remove all the seeds and the stem.

4. Using the spoon, fill the empty part of the apple with peanut butter, adding

raisins. For a bonus treat, include some
M&M'S, too!

5. Wrap in wax paper or aluminum foil for a
great snack after school or practice.

**Elliot and the rest of the team
know lots of fun facts about apples,
peanut butter, and raisins!**

Here are some facts they know:

• Apples float in water because they are made up of 25% air.

• It takes thirty-six apples to make one gallon of apple cider.

• Most kids will eat 1,500 peanut butter sandwiches before they graduate from high school.

• Two U.S. presidents were peanut farmers: Thomas Jefferson and Jimmy Carter.

• Raisins are grapes that have been dried in the sun for two or three weeks.

• More raisins are eaten at breakfast time than any other time of day.

Chip's Super-Helpful Soccer Tips!

Playing soccer is a lot of fun and a lot of hard work! But Chip has some quick tips to help players.

Chip's Tips:

1.   Keep your eye on the ball at all times. Especially when kicking.

2.   Point your non-kicking foot in the direction you want the ball to go. This will help your kicking foot aim better, and the ball will go where you want it to.

3.   Always keep your body between the ball and other players.

4.   Don't forget there are other players on your team. It's important to pass the ball and play with all members of the team. And communicate with your teammates on the field!

5. Be aware of your hands and arms. Remember, only the goalie is allowed to use his/her hands or arms to touch the ball. All other players can use any part of the body except the hands or arms. But be creative — use your knees, shoulders, head, anything!

6. Don't just stand there; move around on the field. Make sure to move to open spots so you're always ready in case the ball comes to you.

7. Wear all protective gear and the proper uniform.

8. Make sure to drink lots of water throughout the game. It's important so players don't get dehydrated. When the body is thirsty, players don't play as well.

Show Your Colors!

It's fun to cheer for your home team, but it's also fun to cheer for your favorite team! One of the best parts of the Walnut Cup for the squirrels is cheering on the different teams. To show support for whatever team you like, you can make a soccer-ball banner.

To make your own soccer-ball banner, you'll need:

- A piece of 8-1/2" x 11" paper (white)
- A pencil
- A pair of scissors
- A grown-up
- Colored pencils, crayons, or markers
- Glue
- A Popsicle stick

To get started:

1. Trace the soccer ball on page 68 on the white paper. Remember to trace all the shapes inside the circle of the ball (these shapes are called hexagons because they each have six sides).

2.   Once you have traced the entire soccer ball, cut out the ball using the scissors. Have a grown-up help you.

3.   After the soccer ball is cut out, color it with your favorite team's colors.

4.   Next, glue your decorated soccer ball to the Popsicle stick. Be sure to let it dry completely!

5.   You now have a banner with which to cheer your team on!

Using the colors of each country's flag, you can decorate your soccer ball banner. Some countries and their colors are listed below, but you can decorate your soccer ball for any country you love!

Germany: red, yellow, and black
Japan: red and white
Spain: red and yellow
U.S.: red, white, and blue
Italy: green, white, and red
Brazil: yellow, green, and blue
Sweden: blue and yellow
France: blue, white, and red

Elliot and his friends
are in for a gusty adventure in
the next Elliot's Park book,
A Windy Tale!

Turn the page for a sneak peek....

The Tumblin' Tumbleweed

"Get ready!" cried Chip. He was holding on to a tree with his front paws. The rest of Chip was in the air, flipping back and forth in the wind.

"This is the windiest day *ever*!" said Elliot, who was holding on just like Chip.

Elliot and Chip were best friends. The two of them watched as a big tumbleweed bounced through Elliot's Park.

"On the count of three!" said Chip.

Chip was a *dangerous* sort of squirrel. He liked to do daring things.

"What did you say?" asked Elliot. The wind made a lot of noise as it passed through the leaves on the trees. It was hard to hear what Chip was saying.

"One . . . two . . . three . . . GO!" yelled Chip. He bumped Elliot with his little squirrel shoulder. Elliot lost his grip on the tree and rolled out into the park. Then the wind died down just enough for Elliot to stand up.

"Here I come!" said Chip. He let go of the tree and tumbled out toward Elliot.

"I don't think this is going to work," said Elliot. "We'll never get home and out of this wind."

Elliot was a safe sort of squirrel. He was not *dangerous* like Chip.

"Sure we will!" said Chip.

The two friends could barely stand up because the wind was so strong. A thousand leaves danced past as Elliot ducked this way and that. But something bigger was coming. It was the tumbleweed, and not just any tumbleweed. Scratchy Spurs, the oldest squirrel in the park, was inside!

"Wow! Scratchy Spurs really can sleep through anything!" said Chip. And he was right. Even with all the noise of the wind through the trees. Even with all the tumblin' inside of a tumbleweed. Scratchy Spurs was still snoring!

"That thing is moving really fast," said Elliot.

"But maybe we can use it to get home!" said Chip. He put his little squirrel paws up to stop the tumblin' tumbleweed. Elliot put his paws up, too. But when the tumblin' tumbleweed hit Elliot and Chip, it kept rolling. It rolled right over the two squirrels and kept on going — with them inside now! But in a different direction!

"Well, that didn't work exactly as planned," said Elliot. "Now we're going the wrong way! Have you got any other ideas?"

Elliot and Chip were rolling head over heels, holding on to the tumblin' tumbleweed. Now there were three squirrels stuck on the ride!

"I haven't seen a storm like this since the old days," said Scratchy Spurs. He had finally woken up and found two visitors in his tumbleweed.

"We're heading straight for that big tree!" said Chip.

"What do we do?" yelled Elliot.

Scratchy Spurs was an old squirrel, but he had also been in the rodeo. He knew when it was time to get off a ride. Scratchy Spurs jumped out of the tumblin' tumbleweed. He did three big rollies in a row and landed behind a nice big rock that blocked the wind.

"Jump!" said Chip. But Elliot was too afraid to jump out of the tumbleweed. Chip didn't want to leave his best friend behind, so they both stayed. The tree was big, and it was getting closer!

The two friends heard a voice from high up in the sky.

"I'll save yoooooooooouuu!"

Looking up from the twisting tangle of the tumbleweed, Elliot and Chip saw who it was.

"It's Crash!" said Elliot.

Crash was the only flying squirrel in the

park. She wore goggles that seemed too big for her head and she had a charming British accent. Everyone called her "crash" because she couldn't land very well.

"Tallyhoooooooo!" she yelled from the sky. But the wind was tossing poor Crash all over. She was completely out of control!

"How is she going to help us from way up there?" asked Chip.

Before Elliot could answer, the tumbleweed hit the tree and *BOoOOooING!* Elliot and Chip flew out of the tumblin' tumbleweed.

"Let's get out of the wind before it tries to blow us away again!" said Elliot.

Elliot and Chip raced through the wind until they came to the big rock. They found Scratchy Spurs. He was in a scratchy sort of mood. He scratched his nose. He scratched his head. He scratched his elbow.

"Look!" cried Elliot.

Chip looked back at the tree they'd just bounced into.

"Where did she go?"

"There! There! There!" It was Twitch, Elliot's sister. She had appeared out of nowhere. She burped a very big, orange-flavored burp. Twitch was the most hyper squirrel in the park because she drank too much soda pop.

"Do you see her? Do you see her?" Twitch was pointing into the air.

Crash had crashed into the tree. She was hanging upside down, her tail stuck between two branches.

"She's flipping and flopping like a sock full of popcorn!" said Scratchy Spurs.

The squirrels stared at Scratchy. They had no idea what he was talking about.

"What'll we do?" asked Elliot. The wind

was howling louder and louder through the trees. Just then the four friends heard a *SNAP* and a *BONK* from somewhere in the park.

"What was that?" asked Chip.

"It's a storm! It's a storm!" yelled Twitch.

Elliot rolled his eyes. "We know it's a storm, silly. I think what Chip meant was the *SNAP* and the *BONK*."

"It sounded like a falling tree," said Chip. "A BIG one."

"Are you okay up there, Crash?" Elliot yelled into the wind.

"Jolly good, mate. Jolly good! I'll be out of this fix in a jiffy."

But Crash couldn't get her tail unstuck no matter how hard she tried. She twisted. She turned. She shook all over. But Crash was still stuck.

Elliot turned to the wise old squirrel of the park.

"What should we do, Scratchy Spurs?"

Scratchy Spurs was curled up in a ball, fast asleep all over again.

"How does he fall asleep so fast?" asked Chip.

"Scratchy Spurs can sleep through anything!" said Twitch, bouncing up and down excitedly.

"I think we better wait here until the storm passes," said Elliot.

Secretly, Elliot was scared. He didn't know what to do. It was the biggest storm ever in Elliot's Park. Something BIG had fallen down. The wind was blowing harder and harder. And Crash was trapped by her tail in a tree!

**For more fun with Elliot
and his friends, check out
www.scholastic.com/elliotspark !**

About the Author
Patrick Carman

Patrick Carman created the world of Elliot's Park while playing with his daughters in their favorite park. When he's not inventing more squirrel adventures for Elliot and his friends, he can be found writing other stories. Patrick is also the bestselling author of the Land of Elyon series, as well as the Skeleton Creek series and the Atherton series. He lives in Walla Walla, Washington, with his family.

Reece Carman and Patrick Carman
with Taffy, the family dog.
Photo courtesy of Reece's older sister, Sierra.
Photo © 2009 by Sierra Carman.